Sonia Zylberberg

The Orange on the Seder Plate:

A mystery in six symbols

The Orange on the Seder Plate:
A mystery in six symbols

© 2012 Sonia Zylberberg
All rights reserved.

ISBN-13: 978-0987789907 (Sonia Zylberberg)
ISBN-10: 0987789902

No part of this book may be used or reproduced in any manner whatsoever without the prior written permission of the author, except in the case of brief quotations embodied in critical articles and reviews.

Any resemblance to actual people is purely accidental.

Book design R. Ftaya.
Cover drawing by Louise Houle.

Original drawings by Louise Houle, except for the egg contributed by Doug Anderson.

If we are indeed more than the sum of our parts, and I believe we are, it is our near and dear ones that make that possible.

In particular, I thank those of my near and dears who participated in the creation of this book: Marilyn Bronstein, Louise Houle, Karen Huska, Vera Kisfalvi, Régine Miller, Devora Neumark, Susan Palmer, Yehudit Silverman, and Diana Yaros.

And especially my dear friend and editor Rose Ftaya.

The six symbols:

    1. Karpas (3)
    2. Maror (19)
    3. Hazeret (35)
    4. Zeroa (41)
    5. Haroset (53)
    6. Beitzah (83)

And a little history:

7. The Orange (87)

She pushed the door open, carefully, tentatively, unsure of what she would find. The note had said come alone, come at once. So she came...

...Inside, all was dark. Except for the unearthly glow coming from the centre of the room. As she came closer she could just about make out the outline of a completely round object at the centre of the light, in the centre of the table. She felt herself falling into the light as it glimmered and pulsated, expanding and shrinking, the rhythm of a heartbeat, but none she recognized.

Closer and closer she came, slowly, tentatively, until her right foot slid on something wet. Regaining her balance, she bent down and felt the puddle on the floor: viscous and thick, it filled her with dread. Retracing her steps, she left quickly, closing the door silently on her way out.

1. Karpas: a plant, usually a green vegetable. It symbolizes spring and rebirth — parsley is most commonly used.

KARPAS

Spring came early that year. The crocuses were already pushing their way through the thawing soil as the heat filtered down into the marrow of her bones, chasing out the lingering winter chill. Bella sat on one of the freshly-cleaned deck chairs, carefully balancing her glass of wine, newly opened to celebrate the unseasonable warmth. On the other chair, her sister leaned back as far as she could, eyes closed against the brilliant sun as she unerringly brought her own glass to her lips and drank thirstily.

"When is the seder?" asked Anna idly. "Have we missed it yet?"

"I don't think so, surely Ma would have mentioned that!" Bella reached for the phone, "Guess we'd better check with her."

"No such luck..." Bella groaned, putting down the phone, "the seder is next Monday. Ma wants to know if Eddie will be coming with you." She said this without inflection, trying to project nothing beyond the literal meaning of the words, trying to filter out her mother's innuendos. No sense in starting the yearly family squabble early – it would doubtlessly start soon enough – Bella sighed to herself.

Anna didn't answer, maybe she really was asleep. Several hours later, when the disappearing sun ushered in the

[3]

cooler temperature, they roused themselves and sat up. "What a gorgeous day," said Anna, stretching her sleepy self. She stood, gathered her purse, sunglasses and cigarettes, said "Gotta go – thanks for the wine" and, before Bella could respond, was gone.

Bella fretted for the rest of the evening: should she have talked to her sister more, should she have tried to get her to talk about the coming seder and Eddie? But Anna didn't seem any readier to talk now than she'd been last year. Or the year before. Things happened to her and she just carried on. Or seemed to. Things like Eddie.

Bella didn't really know much about their relationship and she wasn't anxious to change that. Her interaction with Anna was comfortably superficial: they ate meals, drank wine, and went to the occasional movie. Eddie was never present or mentioned.

It was different in the beginning. Bella had worshipped her older sister, following her around and bringing her little presents, which she now suspected Anna had been too kind to reject: the stone with a sparkling spot of silver, the wildflowers which her mother referred to as weeds, the butterfly wings with their colourful patterns.

But all that changed when Anna reached high school. She became more and more withdrawn, disappeared for long periods of time, and went from being a little reserved to downright secretive. She bought a box with a lock, which she kept under her bed and, eyeballing Bella, forbade her from crossing into her half of their shared bedroom. However much Bella glued herself to the room when Anna was there, she never managed even a glimpse of the inside of that box.

When Anna started staying out later and later, Bella was disconsolate. She waited at the front door night after night hoping, until the last moment, that Anna would be there in time to say good night. But Anna was in a different world, one that didn't include her little sister; she seemed to have forgotten her very existence.

Eventually Bella also started having her own life, her own friends. She also started staying out late and going home only when there was no alternative. In the end, she took no more notice of her sister's presence/absence than Anna did of hers.

Eddie was the first boy Anna brought home. She was nineteen when she introduced him as "the love of my life." At first, Bella was wildly envious of this hunky catch and hung around the couple as much as she could. But, even to her impressionable fourteen-year-old-self, Eddie-the-hunk became much less impressive after a very short acquaintance.

His doting mother had spoiled him and he was accustomed to getting his own way, especially around women. When he didn't, the charm was replaced by petulance and whining. Whatever the attraction was for Anna, Bella quickly lost interest and re-immersed herself in her own life, as far from her family as she could manage. She couldn't remember exactly when Anna and Eddie got married, or even why she didn't attend the city hall event. But at some point, Eddie had become a permanent fixture in their family, or as much of one as the rest of them.

This was after Bella moved out, which she did as soon as she turned eighteen. Since that time, she had spoken to her mother once in a while, seen her less often, and gotten together with her entire family once a year. For the annual seder.

Her brother Carl, exactly one year less a day younger than her, also left home when he turned eighteen. He joined the police force and spent his days patrolling the city and keeping it safe from the forces of evil. Or so Bella imagined. Always quiet, Carl didn't talk much about his work, or anything else. Bella saw him a little more often than she saw their mother, but they were both still more comfortable discussing movies, or even the weather, than anything remotely personal.

A long time ago, probably ten years ago by now, Anna had made overtures to Bella, calling and suggesting they get together. She was trying unsuccessfully to get pregnant and thought that being nice and having more contact with family would improve her chances. Something to do with karma, goddesses, auras, and family links. Bella never got the details straight, but she'd decided she could give being nicer and more family-oriented a try as well. It couldn't hurt her karma! And pretty well anything was more family-oriented than her current life.

The first time, Eddie joined them. That disaster was not repeated. Without his disruptive presence, the sisters found it was not unpleasant to spend the time together. Every few months, they shared a drink, a meal, a movie. Both spent the time "being nice" and, over time, they began to actually enjoy each other's company. Bella even considered bringing up the subject of the locked box, but decided not to jeopardize their fragile relationship.

Anna never did get pregnant. In her desperation she tried every means she heard of: medical, alternative-medical, magical, or completely off the map. It could've been because of her karma, aura, genes, physiology, or maybe it was just plain fate, but the fetus stubbornly refused to materialize.

Eddie did not cope well with Anna's increasing frustration. Even though their encounters were infrequent, Bella saw how the whining increased, the petulance turned nasty, and alcohol became the self-medication of choice. By the time they tried the adoption route, his obvious drinking made failure inevitable. Now, five long years later, they seemed to have settled into .... something .... Bella had no idea what because, along with becoming increasingly desperate in her attempts to achieve motherhood, Anna had also become super-sensitive about her husband. The slightest perceived affront made her hit the roof. So Bella kept her mouth shut and ate, drank, and movied with her sister. Eddie she now saw only at seders.

And these took place with exasperating regularity. Sooner or later, every year, the spring arrived. And brought with it the crocuses, the warm air, and the family Passover seder.

Every year she thought about not going. Every year, she chickened out. Even as she delayed phoning her mother to find out the exact date, she knew she would be there. Each year she hoped it would turn out to be on some impossible night, a night when she absolutely had to be somewhere else. She avoided any calendar on which Passover would be marked, she managed to avoid hearing about the date, but still, somehow, it always ended up on a night when she was available. And search as she might, she could not come up with an excuse that sounded feasible in any way, even to her own eager ears.

It wasn't just Eddie – his presence only made a bad situation worse. Long before he joined their family, it was already an evening to be endured and left behind as quickly as possible. His presence was simply the proverbial straw that broke the camel's back: at some point (five years ago? four years ago?) he had started showing up obviously drunk. That had transformed an annoying evening into an endurance-with-gritted-teeth test.

And that thought flowed into another: her brother Carl's partner, who had transformed the seder in a totally different way. Jake was in many ways the opposite of her strong-silent-type brother. Jake was an extrovert who insisted on sharing his passions and enthusiasms with everyone, which sometimes resulted in an unfortunate tendency to go on and on .... and on and on .... When he did this during Bella's occasional visits, she and Carl waited politely until he ran out of steam and then, after a reasonable interval, began talking about something else. Jake either didn't notice or didn't choose to notice; he just jumped into the new subject with the same abandon.

One of his enthusiasms was for all things Jewish. Coming from a nondescript and mostly secular Protestant-of-some-kind background, Jake LOVED all things Jewish – was sure he had been a Jew in a previous life. Jake wanted to PARTICIPATE, to be ACTIVE, to make Jewishness MEANINGFUL. And he wanted this not just for himself, but for ALL of them. Although he had yet to ask if anyone else wanted it.

It couldn't have been easy for him to join their family. Not only were they not Jewish enough for him, they were positively allergic to *sharing*. Jake trumpeted everything about himself, including his gayness. Carl had been gay from time immemorial, but was so intensely private that Bella wasn't sure if his coworkers even knew he was Jewish, let alone gay.

Although no one in her "liberal" family had ever, within Bella's hearing, mentioned the gay-fact, Jake had to suspect, as she herself did, that her mother and grandfather were not thrilled. She had no idea what her cousin Lila and Lila's husband George thought, but guessed at somewhere between discomfort and outright homophobia. Which left her – Bella hoped she had shown herself as accepting as she felt herself to be – and Anna and Eddie (the most marginal members of a family where everyone inhabited the margins) as a welcoming committee.

Perhaps Jake thought of his enthusiasm as a way to integrate himself into the circle, perhaps his aspirations were more grandiose and he conceived of this as a way to integrate all of them and bring them closer together. For whatever reason, Jake kept on with his relentless enthusiasm, year after year.

Bella didn't understand how he could keep it up when it hit the brick wall of them. Even Carl managed to sit at the opposite end of the table and just about completely ignore him. Whatever their relationship might be like elsewhere, and Bella had seen evidence of it actually being loving and supportive, once they crossed the threshold into the familial ritual arena, Carl abandoned his partner to his own devices.

Bella phoned her brother just to check, but of course he already knew when the seder was taking place. "Is Jake coming too?" just to make conversation: of course Jake would be coming – and doubtlessly even looking forward to it. The only one. Except, maybe, her mother. And of course her grandfather – Zaidy lived for this annual event.

"What's Jake planning for this year?" Every year Jake spent time and more time researching, reading, chatting, emailing, Facebooking and tweeting, coming up with innovation after innovation, hoping to inspire the rest of them with his own discoveries. Every year it was exhausting to sit at the table as he pontificated and pronounced, discoursed and debated, his audience reduced to a glum daze.

"He's on to something new, it's a secret, he won't tell me, he says this way it'll be a surprise for all of us."

"Oh ... is this a good thing?"

"Who knows? At least this way, we're not talking about seders yet." Carl went on: "Is Anna bringing Eddie?"

Ah, the family skeleton rearing its ugly head. If only it could stay safely buried, but not much chance of that. And it would surface soon enough in any case.

"Don't know. Ma asked the same thing, but Anna left without saying."

"I hear he's cleaned himself up."

Bella absorbed this in silence, afraid she had misheard. But when Carl didn't go on, she thought with a small glimmer of hope that maybe she really had heard these long-awaited words. "Where'd you hear that?"

"On the street somewhere." Carl was vague; he had connections everywhere, it was part of his cop-life, a life he managed to keep (mostly) apart and secret. Especially when it concerned his not-so-beloved brother-in-law. But if it was true, this was very welcome news. Eddie high was not a pretty sight. Actually, Eddie not-high was not a pretty sight either, but at least it was a sight more easily stomached (and ignored).

Bella got off the phone and, for the first time, managed to think about the upcoming seder without her stomach ending up in her feet. Even if not the most fun she could imagine, maybe they could get through this year without a tornado.

૨₹

The day of the seder dawned bright and clear. The crocuses greeted the sun with their exhilarating bursts of colour. They inspired Bella's hopes and kept her smiling as she went about her day.

As the evening approached and she remembered where she was going, she faltered. Then she looked at the pot of crocuses in her hands and breathed in deeply, inhaling their riotous exuberance and hopeful attitude: these flowers that made their appearance each spring, rejoicing in the first hint of warmth, ever-hopeful that the freezing cold was, yet again, a thing of the past, and that the future looked bright, brighter, brightest. Fitting partners for the parsley being even now prepared for the seder plate, washed and ready for dipping, symbol of the spring festival that predated the Jews, reaching back to the prehistoric celebration of sap flowing in the earth itself and bursting forth with the spring sun. Green, fresh, screaming out: yes, rebirth is possible! yes, we can change! we have lived through winter and survived! we can rediscover life and joy! we can choose life over death.

Filling herself with the possibility of freshness, she squared her shoulders and, holding the crocuses as a shield in front of her, marched forth.

※

Bella knocked on the door to her mother's house, balancing the pot of crocuses awkwardly in her left hand. "Anyone here?" But she knew she was the first, she was always the first. Try and try as she might, the best she could do was arrive a minute or two late, and that was never enough.

She fumbled to find the key in her overstuffed bag, opened the door and again called out hopefully: "Anyone here?" But no, she could hear the whirring emanating from the kitchen – no doubt her mother, deaf to everything else in her last-minute panic.

Her mother claimed to love these occasions and refused to allow anyone else to bring any of the food. This might have been a good idea if she were a great, or even a competent, cook. Or if she loved cooking. But her culinary expertise was limited to preparing quick meals for one or two people; anything else stressed her severely and she spent the weeks before the seder in a frenzy of non-productive activity.

Somehow she had not yet collapsed from the effort and, even more amazing, every year the meal actually appeared, adequate if not wonderful. She was a person to avoid during this time, a tactic Bella had perfected over the years. A tactic that only and always failed at the last minute, when she seemed incapable of not being the first to arrive.

This year was no exception. The house was empty, except for the whirlwind in the kitchen. And except for Zaidy, of course, who would even now be in his bedroom/dressing room preparing for his role in the evening's spectacle.

In front of her, the enormous table stretched through the living room and dining room, crowding all the usual furniture to the margins. At times like this, her family seemed overwhelming. Was it possible there were only twelve places set? Was it possible there were only twelve of them? Bella felt dwarfed by the table, by the house, by the evening. She felt like Alice in Wonderland after she drank the shrinking potion. She was just thinking how much the Mad Hatter's tea party resembled her family's seder when she was jolted into the present moment by her mother's voice.

"Bella Bella Bella, thank God you're here, I need help, come help me, there's still so much to do and no time to do it where has the time gone, Bella come help me." Bombarded by the rush of words, Bella felt herself swaying dangerously; before she could fall or even turn around, the voice was followed by the flesh and blood person: "What's taking you so long, come help me, Bella didn't you hear me, what's gotten into you tonight, don't you ever think of anyone but yourself? Thank God you're here there's still so much to do."

Hit by a sudden thought, she stopped for a second and looked around. "You didn't bring anyone did you? Thank God, because we'd have to reset the table, that's already done, I did that yesterday, and there's no more room at the table, it's crowded enough as it is, so thank God YOU don't have anyone to bring, but really Bella, you really do

[13]

need to meet someone, you're not getting any younger you know but then we would be thirteen, such an unlucky number although in this case maybe the lucky would offset the unlucky, maybe not, I don't know, but you should find someone."

Another breath and she was off again, "But then maybe you wouldn't always be so early and here to help me thank God you're here to help there's still so much to do and I just don't know where the time's gone and they'll all be here soon, thank God you're here, you're just in time to help."

Bella resolutely breathed in and out, trying to resist the rhythm of her mother's tirade. She had found that was the best way to cope with the onslaught. Pushing the image of her mother as the Queen of Hearts (crying "Off with her head!") out of her mind, she breathed in and out, consciously unclenching her back, her jaws, her teeth, her neck. "Ma," she started to say, "I like living alone." But her mother had already turned away and was listing all the things that needed to be done.

Bella continued with her conscious breathing, trying to reset all the buttons her mother had just pressed. The message that she was selfish, that she was at fault for being early, that she had nothing better to do than help, that she had no life of her own, that certainly she had no life because she had, once again, come alone because she had no partner .... she shook her head to clear out the baggage. There was no point in going there, as she had learned from experience.

"What do you want me to do Ma?"

"The parsley, the parsley, I can't find it, I know I bought it and I don't know where it's gone. It needs to be there, we need something fresh. And green. Find the parsley. Oh my God, we can't have a seder without parsley!"

She was already back in the kitchen, banging pots and drawers as she searched for the parsley. Bella followed and began looking in the fridge. "And the eggs, we need to boil the eggs, get the eggs out too, boil the eggs. And the kids, the kids – what will we do with them? will they get hungry? will they get bored?"

Of course they would get hungry, of course they would get bored. They did every year, why should this year be any different? If anything, they got worse every year. They were old enough and smart enough to remember last year and to know what was coming! Her cousin Lila had three daughters and they were definitely not the seen-but-not-heard kind. Nor the sugar-and-spice-and-everything-nice kind, more like the spitfire-and-demon-children kind. Of course they would get bored, how could they not? SHE would get bored! But, being older by several decades, she was not supposed to show it. They weren't either, but Lila wasn't much of a disciplinarian. George tried, but they mostly ignored him and he, the only male in a house full of women, had stopped making much of an effort. Zaidy, her grandfather, the grand old patriarch (in his own eyes) would growl at them from time to time when he looked up from his haggadah chanting, but this had no effect whatsoever.

Bella continued to search for the parsley. She found it hidden at the back of the fridge, behind the cartons of juice and eggs. Distracted by the vision of her growling grandfather and demon nieces, she mis-negotiated the hazards of the over-stuffed fridge. As her elbow sideswiped an egg carton and sent it crashing to the floor and her foot connected with the viscous mess and her body, inevitably, responded to the pull of gravity, she let out a yowl of frustration. Nothing ever went right on this night! She just wanted to go home!

The moment passed. She slowed down. Breathed. And breathed again. Mopped up the evidence. And returned to her task: the parsley.

Separating the delicate sprigs and washing them in the cool water, she felt herself soothed. Fresh, they called to her, we are fresh! Their smell mingled with the freshness of the crocuses in the dining room: fresh, they all sang out, please, let some fresh air into the seder tonight!

2. Maror: bitter herbs. They symbolize the bitterness of slaves, as experienced by the ancient Hebrew people in Egypt. Horseradish is commonly used.

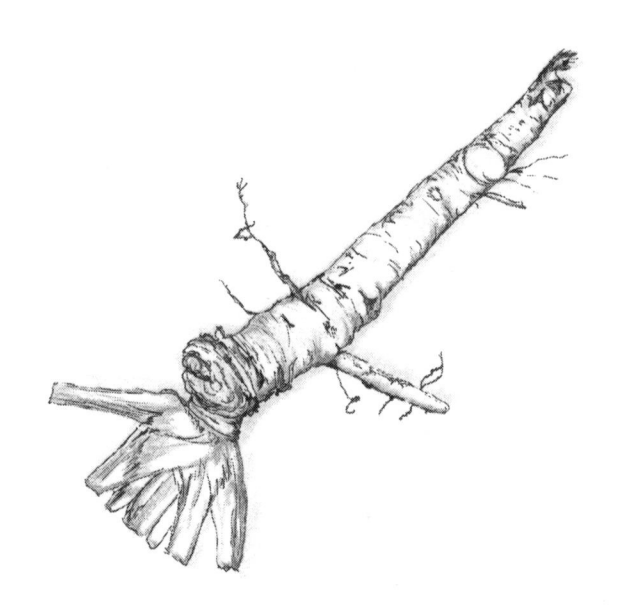

MAROR

Bitterness hung in the air. Bella gazed through the haze of horseradish fumes. She could just about see them rising from the many and extremely large slices of horseradish sitting right in front of her on the table. And, in case that wasn't enough, there was a huge chunk of horseradish on the seder plate in the centre of the table. Was so much bitterness necessary? There was enough here for everyone to taste the bitterness, taste it again, and many more times after that. Bella sighed and tried to breathe in and out calmly and regularly, without choking on the bitterness.

Zaidy sat at the end of the table farthest from her. Once a year, the mild-mannered invisible man disappeared and in his place appeared the patriarch of Zaidy's dreams: a benevolent omnipotent omniscient despot who ruled family and tribe with a will of iron and steel as he led them once again out from slavery in Egypt and into freedom. Striding along beside (or maybe even in front of) Moses, Zaidy held his head high as he wielded the powerful staff, pointing to the sea in the distance. His vision extended further: to the desert on the other side, to the promised land beyond that, to the future without end for him and all his descendents.

Marching to the tune in his own head, Zaidy led the charge of the Light Brigade, the bridge over the River

[19]

Kwai, the landing at D-Day, and every other war movie he had ever watched. Moses, bearing an uncanny resemblance to Charlton Heston in *The Ten Commandments*, deferred to his expertise and wisdom, following where Zaidy chose to lead. The eleven live bodies in front of him were reflected through his magnifying vision into many hundreds, into hords, into armies. The 600,000 Jews who left Egypt were sitting in his dining room as he led the flight to freedom.

He had not, of course, always been Zaidy. A long, very long time ago, he had been little Zalman, a three-year-old on a big boat, holding tight to his mother's hand as they travelled far away from everything they had ever known, on their way to the *goldine medinah*, the land of milk and honey, where all the streets were paved with gold and where a Jew could live a peaceful life, away from pogroms and fear. But Zalman and his mother carried their fear with them and never managed to shake it off.

A distant cousin met them at the port in Montreal, helped them get settled into what was then the bustling and bursting-at-the-seams Jewish community. Zalman's mother never even learned to speak much English or French, getting by with her native Yiddish. But little Zalman went to the local school until he was sixteen. In school and during his working life as a tailor, English was the language he spoke most often. He learned enough French to do business and settled into the tri-lingual life of Jewish Montreal.

He married the girl next door, who moved in with him and his mother. They had two children, a boy and a girl, who went to Jewish afternoon school to learn about their history and traditions.

Zalman's father never made it to the Promised Land. He died in one of the pogroms in the old country, and it was his death that had prompted the exodus of Zalman and his mother.

Zalman remembered his father just a little: he had two images, neither of which ever left him. One was a blurred face kissing him goodnight; the other, a serious and sombre voice telling him to be a good boy.

Throughout his life, he kept these images in mind and did his best to live up to what he thought his father would have wanted. While many of his acquaintances abandoned the traditional practices of their ancestors, Zalman kept them, honouring the memory of his father in the process. Others brought in innovations, changed things, big or small, to make the ancient rituals more modern, more in keeping with contemporary ideas. But Zalman wasn't interested in any of this. If it was good enough for his father, it was good enough for him.

So they kept their home kosher; they joined the nearest synagogue; they celebrated the holidays. If Zalman was ever tempted to sleep in on a Saturday morning, tired from his long week's work, his father's voice started ringing in his head, and he forced himself up and to synagogue for the weekly services. If he was ever tempted to allow the intrusion of any of the changes making the rounds, the spectre of his father appeared, towering above and proclaiming the sanctity of what had gone before.

Now he was an old man. His mother was gone, his wife was gone, his son was gone, and he was retired. He still went to services once a week, and sometimes more often – the synagogue services were just about the only social life he had left. He was tired and spent a lot of time resting, in front of the tv when it was cold and on the balcony when it was warm. Never a large man, he had gotten smaller and smaller and sometimes disappeared into the armchair in the living room.

On Passover all that changed. He expanded in all directions, growing up and out, taking in air and filling the space. He strode instead of walking with faltering steps, he bellowed loudly, he stared boldly at everyone and everything, he glared, he decided, he commanded. He was in charge. All their lives depended on following him. And that meant following exactly. No deviations were tolerated; no exceptions allowed. Absolute discipline was required. Mercilessly, he crushed all opposition, knowing that it was for their own good. This was the only way they could be safe. From his seat at the head, he presided over the table/war zone with an iron fist.

On his right sat George. George was a quiet man. A silent man. With a non-expressive face. There were perhaps places where he opened up, but this was not one of them. Bella had almost never even heard him speak. He tended towards monosyllables. Delivered in a monotone.

Once he had spoken. Perhaps in the mistaken belief that there was a bonding opportunity with his wife's only relatives, he had suggested to her grandfather that they add rice to the foods on the seder table. He started to explain but faltered when he saw Zaidy's look of absolute horror. His words faded away.

George was from Morocco. His Judaism had different rules than Zaidy's East European variety, and one of the big differences was eating rice during Passover. For Moroccan

Jews, this was normal practice. But for Zaidy, rice during Passover was totally FORBIDDEN, a transgression of all that was holy and sacred and godly. His father squirmed in his grave at the very thought. Zaidy couldn't even respond – words failed him and he was left open-mouthed, speechless, breathless, and momentarily even thought-less at the abyss that opened before him.

Bella's mother had stepped into the breach. Picking up the plate of potatoes, she passed them to George with an overly-loud giggle. "Some potatoes, George?" her voice bellowed into the silence. George took the plate silently and that was the last time he spoke up at their table.

Since then, he had attended the seder every year, present but not present, neutral in every way. Sometimes he spoke to his wife or one of his daughters, but rarely. He came, he sat, he ate, he left.

His three daughters were distributed around the table. It was best that way, to keep them away from each other. Free-spirited at best, completely wild at worst, they were little demons dressed in pretty clothes.

Yolly, the oldest, was named for Yolanda, her paternal grandmother, George's mother. When she was born, Nana Yolanda was still alive. Even more than the rice-during-Passover gaffe, this so shocked Ma and Zaidy that they lost all colour and looked ready to collapse.

For East European Jews, this was a travesty, an anathema, a surefire way of bringing the evil eye down on one of the same-named relatives. No matter how much Lila tried to explain it to them, Zaidy especially just kept staring open-mouthed and uncomprehending, white as a ghost.

Lila eventually gave up trying. Anyways, since even

she seemed uncomfortable with it (was this George's one marriage victory? he was easily the most passive person Bella had ever met!), Yolanda immediately became and remained Yolly.

When Molly was born, she was named for Lila's (dead) mother Melinda, but soon became Molly when two-year-old Yolly stumbled over the long name.

And so, inevitably, when Polly came along a year and a half after that, named Sabrina Pearl for the two (dead) grandmothers of her parents, she had no choice but to become the third rhyming sister.

Lila sat between her two younger daughters. Bella slouched down even further into her chair and contemplated her cousin.

Lila was almost as silent as her husband. She had once, long long ago, been lively, happy, talkative, the only child of Zaidy's beloved son, Bella's beloved uncle Sam. But Sam died in a tragic car crash when Lila was eleven. Sam had been loved by everyone and most of all by his daughter.

His death had transformed Lila overnight into a quiet introvert who spoke little and seldom. She had started speaking a little more when her children were born, but only to them.

Lila was older than Bella, about the same age as Anna, and Bella could vaguely remember a time when Lila and Anna played together noisily. But that was when Sam was still alive and Bella's father was still around. Certainly, for the last twenty-five years, Lila had not joined in the seder in any noticeable way or spoken above a whisper.

Now she sat between Molly and Polly, trying to keep them apart and occupied, as they yelled at each other behind her back every time she leaned forward and in front of her every time she leaned back.

Lulled into a semi coma by the heavy atmosphere in the room, Bella sat in isolation at the other end of the table. The chairs next to her were earmarked for Eddie and Anna, in her mother's (usually) vain attempt to keep Eddie in line.

On her other side, at the opposite end from the presiding Zaidy, was the chair where her mother would sit, if she ever did, which she usually did not. The seder was typically accompanied by the banging and crashing caused by assorted disasters in the kitchen. Sometimes Bella got up to investigate; sometimes Carl did; but more often than not they left their mother alone to deal with the latest in a long line of minor crises.

Gita had inherited her father's fears, but without the mantle of invisibility that kept Zaidy from grating on people's nerves. Instead, her near-constant state of anxiety resulted in a barrage of hysterical admonitions, exhortations, complaints, and other assorted irritants. She sat still rarely, the occasional perch at the end of a chair only a momentary pause in her life's journey. When her husband was still around, he often implored her to stop, to sit, but she wouldn't, or couldn't. After he left, no one even tried to keep her still.

By this point, Bella's eyes were almost completely shut and her head was inches away from the table top. A sudden movement stirred the air in front of her and she felt the seat across fill with her brother's body.

Back in the present seder, she smiled a quick hello in his direction. Glancing down the table, she saw that Jake had taken his seat on Zaidy's left. Nodding slightly in that direction, she raised her eyebrows questioningly towards Carl: had he found out Jake's secret plan?

Carl shrugged a no and turned his attention towards the insistent Polly, next to him and pulling on his sleeve. When she had his attention, the five-year-old leaned closer, making him bend down to hear, and started whispering nonstop. Bella heard a few words ("worms", "poop"), enough to realize that Polly was expounding on her latest craze (worm composting) and that she didn't want to hear any more, especially just before dinner. Carl, on the other hand, seemed completely captivated by the conversation.

Bella turned her attention back to Jake. Ah, Jake. A huge smile enveloped his face, he positively glowed with cheerful anticipation. The seat seemed almost too small to contain him as he beamed at all of them, and especially at Zaidy.

Zaidy dipped his head in acknowledgement of the homage he considered his due, then immediately focused on the still-empty seats between Bella and Yolly.

Anna and Eddie had not yet appeared. Perhaps Anna was still trying to sober up her husband. If past years were anything to go by, this was a lost cause. But still, perhaps Carl's information was more up-to-date than hers, maybe Eddie had finally decided to take the sobriety challenge.

Still breathing in the fumes of bitterness, Bella couldn't help remembering seders past, last year's in particular. Anna had tried hard to clean him up, but it was obviously a lost cause. Eddie's glazed eyes followed them through the long readings and even through the meal, with an irrelevant remark and the occasional hiccup making their way out of the fog every once in a while.

They ignored it all. Nothing new here. An intelligent or even relevant remark would have shocked them more. Her mother was obviously doing her best to be civil, to just keep the seder going, doing her best to ignore him, her gaze flitting over him whenever she appeared.

It worked for most of the evening; there was even the hope that they might make it to the end for once. But it was not to be. It was the snore that did it: the loud snore interrupted by the half gulp – result of Anna's under-the-table kick – a second kick, and Eddie's eyes flew open.

Unfortunately, Gita happened into the room at that moment. Stopping in her tracks, she stood and glared at her son-in-law for at least a minute, while everyone else stared at her odd stillness. Everyone except Eddie.

When his eyes began closing again, she asked, in a voice whose razor-sharp edge could have sliced through the hardest diamond, if he wouldn't be more comfortable lying down. Left unsaid, but resounding clearly in the ears of at least her children, was the rest of the sentence "... instead of sitting here with us civilized people!" She had said this so often in the past, it was no longer necessary for her to repeat herself.

Perhaps under the influence of the horseradish she had been inhaling all evening, Anna erupted. "I've had it! I've had enough!! I've had it, had it, had it! You think you're so much better than him! Better than me! Nothing we ever do is good enough!"

And her mother snapped. All the anxiety for the evening, fermented and brewed during the preceding weeks, coalesced and burst out in a diarrhetic spurt, splattering the entire table: "You've had it!!! YOU'VE HAD IT!!! Who's

[27]

the one who's been slaving in the kitchen for weeks, preparing the seder, for weeks now, getting everything ready, just so His Royal Highness over here can show up drunk again and RUIN it, RUIN everything!"

"Who asked you to slave for weeks??????? By yourself!!!!!!! Who asked you to do ALL the work??????? I offered to help, as I offer every year. To help. To cook. To make things, to bring things. So you don't have to do EVERYTHING! But no!! No, no, no! You want to be the one to do everything. To be in charge. In control. To do everything!"

By now, they had progressed from Eddie in particular to life in general and it could only get worse. Anna dredged up events from the past, real and perceived insults to her, to her husband, from seders, from birthdays, from her wedding, from childhood, throughout the 15 years of her marriage, the 35 years of her life, the millennia of Jewish history, all the way back to Egypt and Moses himself. She had always been present, willing, accommodating, helpful, bending over backwards to please, and her mother had never appreciated this, never noticed, never thanked her, never, never, never, and when it came to her husband, it was even worse.........

When she ran out of breath, it was Gita's turn. With no less drama and invective than her daughter, she charged in. "Appreciate what YOU'VE done!! How can you say that to me!!! You ungrateful daughter, and as for your husband: who is it who shows up DRUNK DRUNK!!! D-R-U-N-K DRUNK!!! after I've spent hours and hours and days and weeks!!!" She too went on and on, outdoing Anna's litany, extending back even further in time, before Egypt, back to Sarah and Abraham, back to Eve and Adam.

Bella couldn't quite follow her mother's diatribe, couldn't figure out who was the snake in the scenario, whether it was Anna, Eddie, Anna's (long-departed) father, or her mother's (longer-departed) mother. As their battle hurtled towards its inevitable conclusion, Bella held her breath.

Anna didn't wait for her mother to wind down or even to pause. Grabbing her still-half-asleep-and-dazed husband, she stomped out of the room and the house.

And that was the end of the seder.

Her mother retreated to her bedroom from where the sounds of sobbing and heavy breathing diminished into a silence that permeated the rest of the house.

Zaidy asked plaintively, couldn't they just continue with the seder. He had lost his patriarchal stature and was once again the familiar little old man. No one answered him as they all rushed to leave. Zaidy was left alone with the bitter horseradish remains.

That was last year. And here they were again. They had not been together as a group since then. And, as far as Bella knew, no one had ever mentioned the incident. At least not to her. Perhaps in the privacy of their own home, Carl and Jake, Lila and George, perhaps even Anna and Eddie had spoken about it. But no one had said a word to her or, she was pretty sure, to her mother.

And, of course, the horseradish was present again. An integral part of the seder, a necessary component. Was it her imagination or was there even more of it than usual? She seemed to be seeing everything through the haze of the fumes.

All of them were (so far) on their best behaviour. But of course Eddie and Anna hadn't put in their appearance, the girls hadn't had enough time to become dangerously bored, and the seder hadn't yet begun.

And there was Zaidy, huffing and puffing, straining at the bit, eager to get started in his starring role. Just as the patriarch he had become for the event was about to demand that they begin, the doorbell rang and Anna breezed in with Eddie close behind her. Zaidy lost no time. Waving them impatiently into their chairs, he immediately dove into the ritual reading.

The rest of them examined Eddie as covertly as they could. Anna held herself in until she looked ready to burst. She erupted with "Yes he's sober!" before lapsing back into a brooding silence. Eddie himself reacted not at all, just kept staring into a future where he was not being scrutinized. At least he didn't seem likely to be hiccupping or snoring this year.

Zaidy stopped for a second, startled into a momentary awareness of the contemporary world, miles and millennia away from the mythic time when he was leading the Jews out of Egyptian slavery.

Jake took advantage of the lull. Clearing his throat with great ceremony, he rose to his full five feet seven inches and proclaimed: "I've brought something for the seder plate." Even Carl was staring at him open-mouthed as he reached into his pocket
and
produced
an
orange.
Before any of them could react or stop him, he had placed the orange in the very centre of the seder plate in the very

centre of the table in the very centre of the room, handling it as carefully as a freshly-hatched Fabergé egg.

"It's a new symbol." He launched enthusiastically into his carefully-rehearsed speech. "It represents gays and women and other marginalized Jews ... "

Bella swallowed and swallowed again quickly, greedily sucking air into her lungs in an attempt to keep the laughter from spilling out. For a moment she felt positively giddy from the combination of oxygen and hysteria. It really was very funny – who at the table was not marginal? Poor pathetic Zaidy, emerging from his invisible mantle to imagined grandeur once a year? Or did Jake imagine that Zaidy would join him and acknowledge, maybe even celebrate, his marginalness?

The room had gone very silent with everyone gaping at Jake. Carl had obviously not been given the opportunity to warn him against this heretical act. Jake was not around when George tried to introduce the rice. Jake probably still thought Zaidy would welcome the interest, the fact that someone actually cared about what was going on here. Although, the last three years should have warned him. But Jake was not the most sensitive of souls and was, when he was on a roll, blind and oblivious to all but his own voice. After all this time, Jake had no idea what the old man was like.

Zaidy recovered his voice before the rest of them and started screaming in Yiddish. He screamed and screamed his incomprehensible (to the rest of them) rant. He turned redder and redder as he forgot to breathe, with the string of abuse getting quieter and quieter, although no less vehement, as he neared collapse.

When his voice shrank to a whisper, Gita finally interrupted him. "Dad, do you want to lie down?"

Oh no! shades of ghosts of seders past!

Options for the seder had always been limited: they showed up for the command performance, they played their assigned supporting parts, no improvs, no adlibbing.

Bella dimly recalled Anna asking her own questions, maybe even as far back as when their father was still present, but neither she nor Carl had ever made the attempt. The immediate and absolute rebuff experienced by Anna was enough for them as well.

So they endured, year after year, one of the few efforts they made for the old man or, come to think of it, for their mother.

Then Jake appeared. Jake sat next to the old man, bubbling over with his enthusiasms, adding comments, questions, remarks, suggestions, all of which the old man steadfastly and completely ignored. Well, Jake was not one to be put off by non-reactions. For the last three seders they had endured the battle between Jake's babble and Zaidy's always dominant monotone chant.

Carl always sat at the other end of the table, completely ignoring his partner's enthusiasms. They might just as well have been on opposite sides of the Dead Sea, before Moses parted the waters and let the two sides converge. Every once in a while, Jake looked longingly at his partner, but Carl just would not return the interest. He was so obviously not going there.

This year had begun as usual. Before Jake's bombshell, Carl had seemed completely engaged by Polly and oblivious to the rest of the table. But even Carl, non-engager extraordinaire, could not withstand the shockwaves Jake had set off.

Only Jake himself didn't seem to get it yet. Rather than apologizing or, even better, shutting up, he continued to try and explain. His enthusiasm was boundless. He was not one to be put off by a little sputtering. In Jake's imaginary world, Zaidy stretched out his arms to him and all the others, inviting them to join hands and cry "hallelujah!" Together they would rise, liberated, free at last, one big happy family.

As soon as he could be heard over Zaidy's fading whimpers, he began explaining and explaining and explaining: about the orange, about the marginalized Jews, about the need to be inclusive, about being gay, about the need to re-engage people's interest, about encouraging everyone to participate, about, about, about .... and, of course, it just got worse and worse.

They could all hear the continuing drone as Bella's mother helped her now feeble-looking father to his feet and into his bedroom; the door shut firmly behind them, with an audible click. Then, finally, Jake shut up.

3. *Hazeret*: a second bitter herb that provides an extra dose of bitterness. It may or may not be present; romaine lettuce is commonly used.

HAZERET

"Are you crazy???????!!!!!!!" This from Anna, the least restrained of the siblings. And that started it: everyone else joined in the free-for-all.

In vain Jake explained and protested. He was condemned by all and sundry. No one cared what he had been trying to do. Jake looked baffled by the storm he had provoked. He sputtered: "Carl ... Carl ... " beseechingly to his partner, seeking support. But Carl's determinedly-blank face stared back at him.

As Anna continued to berate him, Jake turned angrily back to face her: "I did this for you. For all of you." Bitterness coloured his words. "Silence is the tool of slavery and oppression – we're free now!"

He turned back to Carl: "I did this for US. For you and me. Don't you see? It's OURS too! Not just Zaidy's! It belongs to us too. WE belong too! WE BELONG TOO!"

Carl refused to engage in the dialogue that Jake was so desperately trying to open. Before Jake could continue, an interruption came from an unexpected corner.

"Why couldn't you leave it alone?" Lila hurled at him. "Why couldn't you just let him get on with it so we could all go home!"

The girls stopped their fidgeting and eyed their mother with interest. In fact, everyone at the table stared with sur-

[35]

prise. This was the most animation Lila had shown in the last twenty-five years – which was well outside the range of memory for most of them. Her reaction to Jake astonished them. Especially her daughters, who had never ever seen their mother acting this way. Their three heads swiveled back and forth as they stared from their newly-unknown mother to the man who had caused this upheaval.

"It's bad enough what he," Lila motioned with her head towards the head of the table from where the absence of Zaidy still dominated, "puts us through every year. Year in and year out and year in and year out. What about us? Year in, year out, we sit and listen to him and listen to him and listen to him."

She focused her fury on Jake. "Why do you have to add to it? Why can't you leave well enough alone!" Lila burst into tears and ran to the bathroom, slamming the door shut after her.

Her daughters turned as one towards the culprit. Under the steady gaze of the six unblinking eyes, Jake wilted.

George looked towards the very-much-closed bathroom door, but made no other move. Bella wondered if he had ever seen his wife act this way. He looked as dazed as the rest of them.

Even Eddie looked mildly interested at the scene in front of him – for once, he was not the object of the yelling, the drama, or even the disapproval.

Bella held her breath, afraid to take in any more of the bitter fumes. The silence lengthened as Jake turned to Carl with one last wordless plea, then shriveled, sinking into the chair which kept him from collapsing altogether.

"Can we eat now?" whined five-year-old Polly. It was late

and she was hungry. She reached for the orange, peeled it and popped a section into her mouth.

The silence continued as they all stared at the peel and listened to Polly chewing. Yolly started giggling. Molly reached for a segment of the orange and popped it into her own mouth, at which point Polly grabbed up the rest of the fruit and shoved it all into her mouth at once.

Carl gathered up the discarded peel and took it into the kitchen. Sounds of garbage can opening and closing. He then continued to the bedroom, knocked gently on the door, opened it and went in.

Anna removed her cigarettes from her bag, got up from the table, opened the back door and went outside to smoke. Bella went into the kitchen and found some dishes to wash. Yolly and Molly started bickering and throwing things at each other. George half-heartedly told them to behave themselves. Eddie stared into space.

Jake just stared at the empty place on the table where, moments before, a glaringly bright orange had sat.

After a while, the door to the bedroom opened. Carl came out first, ushering in the old man. His mother followed a few steps behind. Carl helped his grandfather and mother to their seats. He went to the bathroom and knocked, then through the kitchen to the back door, gathering in his cousin and sisters.

When they were all once again seated around the table, Carl opened his haggadah and motioned to his grandfather to resume. Zaidy picked up where he had left off, his voice a little hoarse and low to start with, but gaining resonance as his self-image flooded back and his spirit returned to ancient Egypt.

The rest of the seder passed with no more eruptions. In fact, with no conversation at all. The haggadah was recited, the ancient story retold. The parsley was dipped into salt water, the fresh greens coated with the saltiness of tears, before being blessed and eaten. The matzah, the bread of affliction, was blessed and eaten. The wine and the meal were consumed. The elephant in the room had disappeared, the orange had been banished.

The event faded into the history of what might have never been. But the bitterness symbolized by the romaine lettuce mingled with the fumes of the horseradish and the family absorbed a triple dose of pungency and rancour that evening. Until, finally, it was over. Bella counted the minutes and finally finally finally fled her mother's home. The freshness with which she had arrived no longer even a distant memory.

Once home, Bella took a very long and very hot shower, trying to wash out the bitter fumes that seemed to have penetrated down to her core. She drank tea, hot and sweet, but that wasn't enough either.

The bitterness seemed to have settled in her bones and she couldn't get rid of it. Was this year really any worse than others? She couldn't remember having had this feeling before, where the bitterness just would not, would not leave. It accompanied her into her bedroom and snuggled in beside her as she turned off the light and made her way to oblivion.

She woke up confused and disoriented to the insistent ringing of the phone. She peered at the clock but it was too dark to make out the time. She buried her head beneath the pillow until the answering machine cut in.

A few seconds later, the ringing started again. Its urgent clamouring penetrated Bella's fog.

"Wha...?" she sort of muttered into the receiver she found in her hand and was jolted into wakefulness by the hysteria pouring out from the phone. "What?" she managed to break into the tirade, "slow down, I don't understand, what are you talking about?"

"His body is lying there, he's dead, oh my God, he's dead, oh my God, what should I do?"

Bella managed to formulate a question: "Who's dead?"

"Dad, my dad, your Zaidy, he's lying in the dining room and he's dead."

"Are you sure?"

"Yes, of course I'm sure! he's not breathing and he's lying on the dining room floor and what should I do oh my God he's dead what should I do ... "

" ... try and breathe. Go lie down, I'll be right over." Even as she heard herself mimicking her mother's remedy for all upsets and difficulties, Bella hung up the phone and started dressing with one hand, while the other dialed her brother's number. Carl the cop would know what to do.

4. *Zeroa:* shank bone, usually from a lamb. This bone is not used in any ritual, but its presence serves as a reminder of the ancient Passover sacrifice.

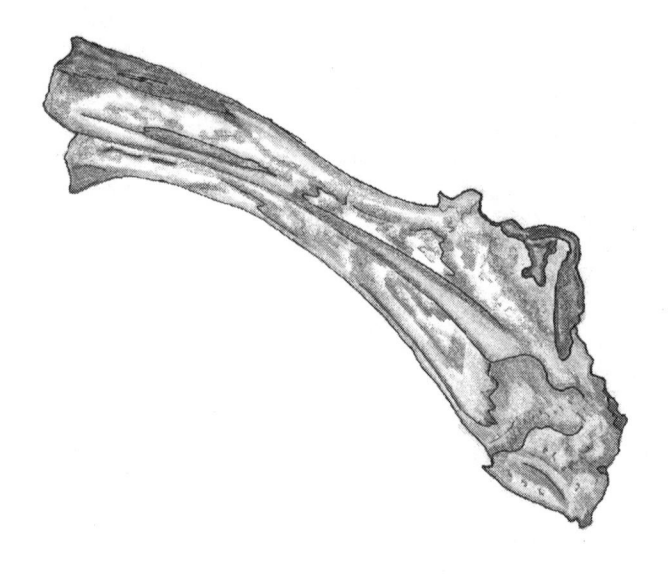

ZEROA

Bella collapsed on the couch. She'd brought her still-hysterical mother home with her and had finally managed to get her to bed. Thank god for modern medicine; the sleeping pill was taking hold and her mother was drifting off.

"You see," she yelled silently at Gita, "it's good that I live alone so I can give you my bed so easily!" But the Pavlovian reflex was half-hearted and she found herself with more sympathy than she could remember ever having had for the woman who lay there sleeping and who had looked so very lost, clinging to a daughter for guidance and support.

She put some sheets on the couch, lay down and turned off the light. What seemed like seconds later, she was awake, in a cold sweat, battling terror.

She had pushed the door open, carefully, tentatively, unsure of what she would find. The note had said come alone, come at once. So she came ...

... Inside, all was dark. Except for the unearthly glow coming from the centre of the room. As she came closer she could just about make out the outline of a completely round object at the centre of the light, in the centre of the table. She felt herself falling into the light as it glimmered and pulsated, expanding and shrinking, the rhythm of a heartbeat, but none she recognized.

Closer and closer she came, slowly, tentatively, until her right foot slid on something wet. Regaining her balance, she bent down and felt the puddle on the floor: viscous and thick, it filled her with dread. Retracing her steps, she left quickly, closing the door silently on her way out.

Now, in the absolute darkness of the unfamiliar living-room-as-bedroom, she could not shake off the dread that had accompanied her in the dream. She tried to go back to sleep, but the voices in her head took over. Zaidy was dead. Zaidy was dead!

She tossed and turned, turned and tossed. Perhaps the bitterness would never leave now, nothing would ever get rid of it and she was doomed to live with it as a constant companion. That certainly fit with her dream. The dream – what was she to make of it?

Nothing? The aftereffect of a lousy seder with too much food. The everpresent bitter fumes. Zaidy's death. But she could not rid herself of the feeling that there was more to it, that the dream *meant* something. That it was a message. For her. But how could that be? a message from whom? and, if it was a message, what was she being told? and why?

Bella was not usually in touch with spirits or the spirit world. She didn't think she even believed in ghosts. Where, who, what, how had it come to her?

When she was very young, long before her grandfather had come to live in their house, while his wife and her father were still around, she had been entranced by the old man. In a special story-telling voice he had recounted tales of miracles, of angels, of dybbuks, of ghosts. Stories of biblical ancestors who walked and talked with God and of more recent visionaries and miracle-workers. Stories of glory and tragedy and even a little comedy. But, over time, the story-telling had tapered off and eventually disappeared. Bella could not even remember the child who had sat at Zaidy's feet and listened to them.

Was her dream a throwback to those stories? Was it a message from beyond the grave? Bella's head whirled, dizzyness and exhaustion sucking her into a spinning vortex of meaningless chaos.

The reality was that Zaidy was dead. Not ghost or spirit or dream, but the actual flesh and blood old man. The death was a tragic accident, nothing more. Carl had met her at the house along with the official personnel and assorted paraphernalia. And, while they had to wait for the autopsy to confirm it, they all agreed that it looked like the old man slipped on a small puddle of orange juice on the floor. Falling, he hit his head on the corner of the table which still overfilled the room, and died from the injury. End of story. End of report. End of a life.

Once the two (old man and puddle) were together in the room, their meeting was probably inevitable – the large table left very little room for manoeuvering. Not known was why he was in the room at all. Also not known: where had the puddle come from? But she was the only one asking those questions, the only one who was uneasy.

Carl looked exhausted as he brushed her off: he just wanted the whole thing to be over so he could go home to bed. She didn't bother to ask the official investigators – if his own grandson wasn't interested, it seemed unlikely they would be. If not for her dream, she probably would have let it go herself. But she wasn't about to share her dream-experience with her solidly down-to-earth brother.

Zaidy had looked so small in death. Even smaller than his usual shrunken self. Completely vanished was the omnipotent patriarch. In his place such a small corpse.

"Zaidy," Bella implored as she stopped trying to force sleep to come to her, "are you there?" She didn't know how one usually went about talking to spirits but she was desperate. She closed her eyes and tried to picture Zaidy as he'd been when alive. But all she could see was that shrunken corpse. "Zaidy's ghost, are you there?" There was no answer, not even the slightest shiver down her spine.

The image of his corpse stayed with her. So little at the end. But in fact he had always been little, on the outskirts of their lives.

They'd mostly ignored him, certainly as far back as she could remember; even her mother, who had eventually brought Zaidy to live with them. Bella couldn't remember any of them having a conversation with the old man ... or trying ... except, of course, for Jake ... and George ... and Lila ... and Anna ....

As she thought back over the years, Bella had flashes of Zaidy with the other family members. The scenes played out rapidly and silently. Bella couldn't actually focus the images, but everything looked unpleasant and hostile, with angry pinched faces confronting each other. There seemed to be a lot of yelling going on, from Zaidy of course, but it looked like all the others were shouting as well. The only person, besides herself, missing from these scenes was Carl – either he had never actively clashed with the old man, or else not in Bella's presence.

Anna certainly had. As her interior movie continued to roll, the sound kicked in, and Bella re-discovered many occasions on which she had witnessed clashes between her sister and grandfather: at the table over soup, over brisket, over dessert, glaring matches which poisoned whatever food they were trying to eat. In the backyard, a nineteen-year-old Anna screamed at the little man: "Just stay out of my life, OK!!!!!!!" "But how can I do that? You have no father to look after you, you need a man to look after you – men know about these things. Someone has to watch over you and keep you from doing what is wrong, what is shameful." "I'm old enough to look after myself. And I DO have a father. I certainly don't need you spying on me!" Anna delivered her parting torrent and stomped off.

Bella sat up abruptly. Had she fallen asleep? What brought that back? She'd worked hard to forget that period of her life. The summer that Anna was nineteen, she, Bella, had been away most of the time.

Her father had left the year before, lured away by the illusion of youth in the person of a twenty-year-old blonde dog-trainer. Her devastated mother alternated between work and sick-bed. Bella and Carl were shipped off to the farm of a distant cousin, where they learned to milk goats and to hide and to watch. On their infrequent visits back home, they dropped the milking, but continued to hone their other skills, discovering better and better hiding places into which to squeeze their growing bodies. Hiding and watching – sometimes Bella wondered if that was why Carl had become a cop.

Anna avoided their fate by finding herself a job for the summer, working at the local coffeeshop for a pittance and tips. She had obviously been doing more than that, although Bella had no idea what. Apparently Zaidy did, though. Bella tried to imagine the old man spying on her sister, but the image of Zaidy as Sherlock Holmes didn't quite fit. More likely he had done it with his usual incompetence, which was how Anna found out what he was up to.

Why had that image come to Bella? She'd avoided those memories for years. And, probably, so had the rest of her family. They certainly never talked about them! The departure of their father had left the whole household on edge and they had basically stopped communicating. She and Carl, allies in hiding, had talked a bit, but mostly about how to find more and better hiding places.

Bella leaned back on the couch and closed her eyes again. Her movie continued: this time Eddie filled the screen. When she and Carl had returned at the end of the summer, Eddie was already around. Was that what Zaidy had discovered? Eddie at the time was inoffensive – at least compared to his future self. Could ineffectual little Zaidy have had a premonition of the loser Eddie would become? The scene she was watching was of an older Eddie, obviously drunk, slurring his words and holding on to the sofa for support.

"What business is it of yours what I do with MY wife??????? Just butt out, OK???????" So close together that they looked about to butt heads, Eddie spat this invective at his grandfather-in-law. The little old man took a step back and shook his head along with his finger in Eddie's face: "But she's my granddaughter. And she has no one else to look out for her." "She has ME, OK??????? Now just BUTT OUT!" Zaidy wouldn't take this for an answer: "But you need to stop drinking, then maybe you would have more luck with the adoption ... " But again Eddie erupted, showering the air between them with his rage: "BUTT OUT!" and stomped off.

Bella sat up with a jerk. Had she fallen asleep again? The Zaidy she was seeing was not her old familiar grandfather – this one tried, however ineffectually, to direct and protect his family. But it wasn't going over very well – Anna and Eddie, at least, seemed to prefer the privacy of their self-created misery.

What about her mother? After the abrupt departure of her husband, Gita had brought her widowed father to live with her. Besides helping with the mortgage, maybe she also hoped he would help her with the three children. She had been so overwhelmed and frightened, so alone. Bella's father had preferred to forget that he was a father, to forget the reality of Anna, Bella, and Carl – he vanished from their lives, completely.

Before that time, Zaidy had been an occasional visitor, at first with Bubbie, then by himself. He came, he sat, he drank tea, he went home. After, he came and stayed; he moved in; he stayed. And, leaned on by his daughter, he tried to become a pillar of support.

Bella had, mostly, avoided him. Those hiding lessons on the farm served her well and she managed to live her life out of the range of perception of her mother and grandfather. Carl also seemed to be quietly doing what he wanted. Maybe Anna would have profited from spending the summer with her siblings!

Now Bella saw her mother locked in battle with Zaidy. "It's not my fault, it's not my fault, IT'S NOT MY FAULT!" "He was a good husband – what did you do to him?" What was Zaidy trying to do here? Was he blaming her mother? "You must have done something – men don't leave for nothing. Not with three children and a job and house and family." "Go and ask him yourself, if you can find that good-for-nothing. I tried my best." "Your best wasn't good enough." Her mother cried and cried, but Zaidy was relentless: "This is just a phase – all men go through such a phase. You need to put your pride aside. Go and find him, get down on your knees to him, beg him to come back where he belongs." Gita cried and cried and turned away from her father.

Bella wanted to reach in and strangle the old man. Who did he think he was? Couldn't he see the people right in front of him? He seemed to have a knack for saying the wrong thing, the one most guaranteed to hurt and close off any possible communication.

The scenes with Lila followed this pattern. Lila, usually so silent, seemed to have found her voice when her grandfather wanted her to mourn her father in the traditional ways. "He's dead, OK? He's dead, he's gone, you can't bring him back, you can't pretend he's still here, he's just gone!" "We can honour his memory, we can ... " Lila cut Zaidy off: "Talking endlessly about him doesn't honour anything, it just makes me miss him and miss him and miss him." "That's why we need to honour his memory ... " "But I miss him too much, I can't stand this!" "We need to light candles for him, we need to go to synagogue on his yahrzeit, we need to ... " "You do what you like, I'm not doing anything!" "But you are his daughter, YOU need to ... " "I don't need to do anything! Leave me out of your plans!" And Lila ran out of the room.

George's scenes were calmer, but no less antagonistic. Here Bella's soundtrack seemed to be malfunctioning – or maybe it was that the sound itself was entirely one-sided. George's mouth remained firmly closed as Zaidy lectured him on his duty as son-in-law to his wife's dead father. "You need to ... you must ... you are obligated ... you must ... you must ... you must ... " George appeared to have fully integrated the lessons of the rice incident: silence and passive resistance were his only response.

Even the rhyming sisters had managed to clash with Zaidy. Bella watched as first Yolly, then Molly, and finally Polly made faces and stuck out tongues behind the back of the old man remonstrating feebly at them to behave themselves. They had even managed to have words with him. When her great-grandfather told her she was too old to be running around in such a state, and that she should begin to act like a young lady, Yolly told the shocked old man to fuck off. Molly, entering the room in time to hear this response, erupted into giggles and gleefully told him where he could stick his advice. Polly, never far behind her sisters, slid into the room and added a few choice terms. Then, before Zaidy could recover his ability to speak, they stuck out their tongues, let out a victorious shriek, and zoomed out of the room.

And Jake? Jake never had a chance. He'd actually looked forward to meeting Carl's family – his enthusiasm for all things Jewish led him to believe that he would find a traditional home brimming with folksy language, food, customs, and warmth. He breezed in behind Carl, bearing smiles, chocolates (kosher of course, even though no one in Bella's family, except Zaidy, cared), and flowers.

Bella's mother did try to live up to Jake's expectations, at least at first. But Zaidy, right from the start, reacted badly. Jake made him nervous; the expectation that he would discuss his traditions, his practices, that there would be dialogue, did not sit easily with the old man. So he answered all Jake's overtures irritably and curtly, not even meeting Jake partway. The final clash, of course, had been that very evening, when Jake, after three fruitless years of trying for discussion, had seized the initiative and placed his orange on the seder plate without consulting Zaidy beforehand. The results of that had sent Zaidy to bed and finally shut Jake up.

By now Bella had stopped wondering why her memory had lost its habitual amnesia; she just sat, watching in stunned bewilderment. Whether stimulated by the evening's drama, or by her sense that something was not quite right about his death, or by a spooky message from a now-dead-Zaidy still trying to lead the way, her film showed her grandfather in confrontation. With everyone. Of all her family, only she and Carl were absent. She drifted into a fitful sleep.

And woke suddenly from another dream. This time Zaidy raged from a spotlighted centre, surrounded by growling lions which he kept at bay with his serpent-staff. While one part of her marvelled at how her Jewish-school lessons had stuck to the back of her brain for so many years, another part regarded the image of Zaidy-as-Moses and wondered how, for such an ineffectual person, he had managed to wield such power. To get them all, every year, to re-assemble for their annual painful and pain-filled re-enactment!

Even Bella, who had avoided conflict with her grandfather, hated those events. Yet she had faithfully dragged her reluctant self there every year. Anna, Eddie, Lila, George, Gita, even the rhyming sisters, all of whom had suffered Zaidy's clumsy intrusiveness, must have hated the seders at least as much. But they came, they endured, sometimes silently, occasionally hysterically; each year they arrived, a steady procession of sacrificial lambs, to be offered on the altar of one lonely old man's desire to be a good man, a good father, a good grandfather, a good leader, an honour to the memory of his father and to Moses.... Bella finally fell asleep counting the sacrificial sheep.

5. Haroset: a sweet paste made from wine and spices, fruits, nuts, honey and/or date syrup, symbolizing the mortar from which the Hebrew people made bricks during slavery. Often eaten together with the maror to create a bittersweet reminder: the sweetness of freedom tinged with the memory of the bitterness of slavery.

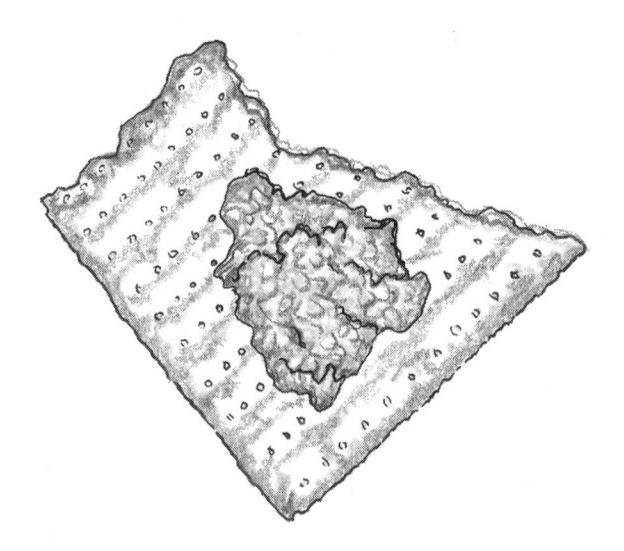

HAROSET

Bella sat on the couch between her brother and sister, trapped in the shiva ritual, all of them nodding in unison at the appropriate moments as a previously-unknown crony of Zaidy's droned on with remembrances spanning sixty years. Bella had lost the thread around year forty and was sure Anna was sleeping.

She so envied her sister's ability to sleep with eyes open and head nodding. Anna had learned the trick in grade school and tried to teach her little sister, but Bella had never managed it. So she was stuck with daydreaming.

God, she was tired. The long day had started with coming over to her mother's to help prepare for the after-funeral reception, then the funeral service at 11, followed by the graveside burial, then hurrying to get back to her mother's before any of the guests showed up.

Too many people, too many things to see to. In theory, the family didn't have to worry about material concerns during the period of mourning, but somehow there she was, setting out food: the gap between theory and practice!

She had managed to stay polite and appear sociable all day but her patience was wearing thin. If Zaidy's friend (what was his name anyway? Sam? Saul?) didn't shut up soon, Bella was afraid she was going to blow. She stood up abruptly, said "Excuse me" to the startled crony, and left her siblings to deal with him. She practically ran to the bathroom which was, thankfully, unoccupied, locked the door, and sank onto the toilet. Ah ... peace, blessed peace.

She closed her eyes (just for a moment, she promised herself) and there was ... Zaidy ... dressed in his white shroud ... glaring at her accusingly. Bella felt a huge wave of guilt engulf her. She had managed to push all questions surrounding the death out of her mind.

In any case she had been much too busy – the Jewish custom of burying the dead as soon as possible had resulted in two days of insane activity. With her mother nearly paralyzed by shock and grief and with Anna conveniently absent, the load had fallen on her and Carl. Somewhere in the rushing around and planning frenzy, Bella had tentatively broached the subject with her brother. Carl's response was unambiguously and completely dismissive.

As she quickly opened her eyes to banish the unwelcome ghost, a sweet smell assailed her. The pastries had not seemed so overwhelming earlier, now their cloying sweetness carried an underlying bitterness. The combination nauseated her. Here they were, in the house of mourning and Bella could not rid herself, try as she might, of the bitterness of the seder night; it had insinuated itself deep inside her, and attached itself to every other smell or taste she came into contact with.

A knock on the door roused her and she abandoned the relative tranquility of the bathroom. Reentering the living room, she saw that all the guests had left, only her family remained.

Her mother still sat on the low chair that brought mourners closer to the ground in which the dead were laid to rest. Jake sat next to her, offering comfort and tea. Her own place on the sofa had been taken by Lila with Polly asleep on her lap. Anna and Carl flanked her, Anna's eyes still open whereas Carl's were now closed. Molly and Yolly lay at their mother's feet, idly pushing a few marbles back and forth. George sat on one of the chairs by the window and Eddie, coming in from the bathroom, joined him there.

There was silence. Molly broke it briefly with a triumphant yelp as she reached under the couch and pulled out a large marble, then lapsed back into an uncharacteristically subdued game with her sister.

Bella sank onto the closest chair. As she surveyed the room, she saw that Zaidy had reappeared and was floating between her and the others. And he (or was it an "it"?) was looking directly at her, pleading – please please Bella – it seemed to say – do something. About what? she silently demanded – what do you want of me?

He continued to implore, increasing the intensity of his gaze, until Bella couldn't stand it.

"How did that orange juice get on the floor anyways?"

Her question sounded much louder and more aggressive than she had intended. Everyone jumped, eyes snapped open, heads turned towards her. With all that attention on her, Bella felt she had to continue: "Well, don't you find it a little strange?"

The silence lengthened.

"And what was Zaidy doing in here at that time of night?"

Her mother's sobbing broke in. "It's all my fault – I killed my own father!"

Ten heads swiveled towards her as she continued to sob. Brushing off Jake's proffered arm of sympathy, she groped for the box of tissues and blew her nose loudly.

"What are you talking about, Ma?" Carl's voice cut through the collective gasps. "It was an accident."

"I was distracted that night – I cleaned up but I wasn't paying attention. And then I took my sleeping pill and went to bed. I didn't finish. He always said that I never did anything right. It's my fault!"

Gradually her ramblings became a little more coherent and Bella realized her mother was not claiming to have actually killed Zaidy, but only of having neglected to mop up the spilled juice. "But," she interrupted, "where did the juice come from in the first place?"

Her mother stopped mid-sniffle, "Well, I guess it got spilled."

"But," Bella persisted, "when? We weren't drinking orange juice."

"Well, someone must have been."

Bella looked inquiringly at the rest of her family, "Who was drinking orange juice?" No one answered. She looked at the girls: "Any of you?" They all shook their heads and Lila answered for them, "No, they all had grape juice. Because it was Passover. Purple grape juice," she added, just in case anyone thought it could have been mistaken for orange juice.

"Grape juice for me too," this from Eddie, somewhat sheepishly. At any other time, Bella would have been amazed at this revelation from the (could it possibly be former?) alcoholic, but she was focused on a different issue right now.

One by one, each family member said what they had been drinking: wine for everyone else, except Carl, who had stuck to juice because he was on call. No one claimed the orange juice.

"Couldn't it have come from Jake's orange?" Carl asked, somewhat reluctant, it seemed, to mention the gone-but-hardly-missed addition to the seder plate.

"But Polly ate it," Bella replied, "and pretty fast. I don't remember any juice spilling." Polly nodded in agreement, "No way I spilled." Lila reinforced her daughter's innocence, "She's very good that way, never makes a mess, she never has, not even as a baby." Polly beamed proudly and Molly pinched her. Lila turned back to her children as Polly burst into screams and curses.

"How about after the meal?" Bella persevered. "Did anyone have juice after the meal?"

Silence.

"Was there even juice in the house?" Bella asked.

Her mother nodded: there was a carton in the fridge.

"Maybe we should dust it for fingerprints!" Anna suggested jokingly. But Bella turned eagerly to her brother.

"Could we do that?"

Without waiting for his answer, she ran into the kitchen and yanked open the door of the fridge. There was no carton of juice staring back at her. Thinking she had missed it in the overflowing mass of foodstuffs, she looked through every shelf carefully and methodically. No juice.

Coming back into the living room, she addressed the waiting crowd: "Did anyone finish the juice?" Silence. "Did it get put out today for the funeral?" Silence. "Did anyone see the carton?" Still nothing but silence.

"Am I the only one to find this a little suspicious?" Bella's eyes flicked to the cop in the room, who looked as if the bitterness of the situation had just exploded in his mouth.

"Maybe someone just forgot?" he suggested slowly.

When there was no answer, he got up and went into the kitchen. Bella heard the back door open and then close as Carl went out to see if the garbage was still there. She knew it was not – the trash can had been empty when she took out the garbage earlier in the day. Unless it was in that bag? She went out to join her brother and share this information with him.

She found him leaning against the back door staring into the garbage can in which it was clear there was no carton of any kind. "It doesn't mean anything," Carl said. "Of course not," Bella replied.

They both continued to stare at the sad little pile of garbage. "Recycling?" she asked half-heartedly, knowing in advance what the answer would be. Sure enough, Carl pointed at the empty recycling bin behind her.

When they went back inside, they found everyone gone except for Jake, who was helping their mother clean up. Carl kissed his mother goodbye and gestured to his partner to come. Bella heard them leaving as she took over the clean-up duty.

"You must be exhausted," she said to her mother, "sit down and I'll make you some tea."

Her mother didn't argue, simply sank into a chair and closed her eyes. Either last night's sleeping pill was still lingering, or the flood of emotions had succeeded in calming the constant movement; in any case, she was stiller than Bella had ever seen her.

Bella brought the steaming cups to the table and sat down next to her mother, whose eyes opened as she reached for the tea. "Did you even see the juice on the floor when you were clearing up?" Bella asked her. In reply, her mother closed her eyes again.

Just as Bella was wondering if she needed to wake her up, her eyes opened abruptly: "I don't think so," she exclaimed excitedly, "I don't think there was any juice. I don't think it was there!"

※

Sister
The next week, Bella casually dropped by her sister's house after work. A slippered and aproned Eddie opened the door and stared at her, open-mouthed. Bella tried not to do the same back at the domestic vision in front of her: "It's not like I've never been here before," she said by way of greeting, aiming but not quite achieving a humorous tone. "Can I come in?"

Eddie stepped aside and, in a voice that could not quite hide the astonishment, called to Anna that her sister was there. Anna came running.

"What's the matter? Is Ma okay?"
"Everything's fine. I just wanted to talk to you guys."
They both stared at her.
"About the night Zaidy died."
They still stared.
"In case you remembered anything."
"About what?" This from Anna.

"About anything – the juice, the others … " Bella's voice trailed off. This was weird, questioning her family as 'witnesses' (and/or possibly suspects?), but she ploughed on, determined to continue.

"Maybe you could just tell me what you do remember? Just in case there's anything you forgot or didn't notice at the time?"

Anna led the way to the kitchen, where Eddie plugged in the kettle. Bella decided to match their nonchalance and not remark on the new domestic version of her brother-in-law.

As Eddie placed a teapot on the table in front of them, she also decided not to comment on the choice of drink. As if reading her mind, Anna said, "No alcohol in the house" and poured the tea.

They both looked at Bella.

"Well," Bella started hesitantly, "tell me about the end of the evening. Did you leave right after the meal? I was doing dishes in the kitchen, by the time I got out of there everyone was gone."

"Well," said Anna after a few moments, "I was helping Ma clear the table, I brought you the rest of the glasses."

"I remember," said Bella encouragingly.

"Then I saw Eddie coming out of the bathroom and figured we'd better go home."

Bella turned to Eddie.

"I spent the whole time in the bathroom. From when we finished til we left."

Bella could think of nothing to ask him that wouldn't sound, at the very least, indelicate. Whatever he had been doing in the bathroom all that time would just have to remain his secret unless he offered to share. She thought to herself that she wasn't a very good detective.

"Do you want anything else with me?" Eddie asked and, when Bella said no, disappeared into the living room from which the sounds of the tv set emerged.

Still trying to reconcile this new Eddie with the old one, Bella turned to her sister: "What's with Eddie?"

Anna shrugged. "He hit bottom. So now he's trying to atone."

"What did he do?" Before Bella could bite her tongue, the question had escaped. She could only manage so much delicacy with her family on such short notice!

"He shoved a pregnant woman who butted in in front of him in the supermarket checkout. Luckily, she went into labour instead of miscarrying."

"Oh."

"He doesn't remember any of it because he was so drunk."

"Oh."

"She's decided not to press charges."

Belle let her eyebrows do the oh-ing this time. She could think of nothing at all to say. The lack of inflection or emotion in Anna's voice did not encourage sympathy, pity, or anything else.

After a moment, she cleared her throat, took a sip of tea, and returned to the seder night.

"Did anyone leave while you were clearing the table?"

"Mmmmmmm ... I was kind of preoccupied with trying to figure out where Eddie was and what he was doing and at the same time avoiding Ma's eye so she couldn't ask." Anna took a gulp of the tea which was now close to room temperature. "But I think Lila and family may have gone, it got quiet at some point."

"Did you maybe open the fridge at all? To put food away?"

"Nnnnnnno, I don't think so, Ma was doing food, I was just doing dishes."

"Was Carl still around when you left? and Jake?"

"I didn't see them." Anna started suddenly, "Oh, but wait a sec, they must have still been there, their car was behind mine and I almost hit it getting out because it was such a tight squeeze."

"Thanks Anna." Bella realized as she kissed her sister goodbye that this was the most personal conversation they had had in years. Sad that it took the death of Zaidy to make it possible.

She decided not to disturb Eddie just to say goodbye but thought, as she left, that maybe she would come by again at some point soon.

Cousin
When she dropped in on Lila the next day, the astonishment was, if possible, even greater and more apparent. Lila gaped at her from the doorway.

"Hi Lila," Bella said as casually as she could. "Can I come in?"

It was true that she had never been to her cousin's house before. She had even had to look up the address in the phone book.

Lila recovered a little and abruptly motioned her in, closing the door carefully behind her. Bella walked over and around the assortment of shoes, jackets, toys and other stuff in the entranceway and emerged into the living room. Lila was more hostile than Anna and Eddie had been, she eyed Bella aggressively as she waited for her to explain the unprecedented visit.

Bella cleared her throat and, trying not to sound as nervous as she felt, smiled at her cousin.

"The girls aren't home?"

"Did you want to see them?" Lila asked in surprise.

"Well, not exactly," Bella stammered. "Well, yes, actually. I wanted to talk to all of you."

When Lila just kept looking at her, she continued, "About the other night."

"Are you still going on about that? What is the matter with you? Give it a rest!"

"But it *is* strange, think about it, it doesn't make sense."

"Sure it does. Zaidy slipped, banged his head, and died. End of story."

Bella sighed, "OK, OK, but humour me."

"In what way?"

"After dinner, what did you do? Between the end of the meal and you leaving. How long did it take you?"

"As long as it takes to gather up three children, all their belongings, socks, jackets, IPods, toys ... and get out the door. And not a minute longer." Lila thought for a moment. "Maybe ten minutes."

"Were they all with you the whole time?"

"No, they were looking for their things. All over the house. That's how kids are – they drop things, everywhere. Polly couldn't find one sock. And Molly never did find all her marbles."

[63]

"Were you in the kitchen at all?"
"No, I don't think so."
"Were the girls?"
"I don't think so."
"What about George?"
"*What* about George?"
"Was he with you?"
"No, of course not."
"Where was he?"
"I have no idea. Wherever he always disappears to."
"Well – how did you find him eventually?"
"I texted him and he met us at the car."

Bella persevered through her cousin's short-as-possible answers: "Did he come from inside the house? Was he at the car before you?"

"I don't think so."

Bella sighed as she realized her cousin's pig-headedness was forcing her to be much more precise than usual: "You don't think he was there before you? or you don't think he came from inside the house?"

"I don't know."

Bella, increasingly frustrated with Lila, was trying not to show it, in case she pushed her cousin over the edge into total non-cooperation. The rapprochement she had experienced with her sister was definitely not being repeated with her cousin. Maybe she would have better luck with the kids.

"Can I talk to the girls?"

"I guess ... " Lila's reluctance was tangible, but after a moment she shrugged. "Why not? It might keep them entertained for a while."

And, in fact, the girls were much more interested than their mother had been. The idea of playing detective appealed to all three of them. They immediately started competing to see who could remember the most. As they vied for her attention, Bella tried to get them to talk one at a time.

Lila looked on, interested at last, but only in watching as Bella floundered in her effort to impose some kind of order. She made no move to help. The noise and chaos increased until Bella, out of sheer desperation, put her hands over her ears and closed her eyes.

Gradually she felt a lessening of the bedlam and eventually, when she could hear nothing, cautiously opened one eye. Six intense identical brown eyes stared back at her and three mouths opened in unison as, hawk-like, they registered the change.

Quicker than them, she shut the eye and waited again. When she tried opening an eye several minutes later, the six unblinking eyes still stared at her, but this time the mouths didn't move. She opened the other eye slowly and, when the mouths remained closed, slowly lowered her hands. With her ears once again uncovered, she held up a finger and said quietly:

"One at a time."

When the three mouths opened simultaneously, she again held up a finger.

"Put your hand up when you want to talk."

Three hands shot up.

Bella had no idea how to handle this. She looked at Lila for guidance, but her cousin was still looking on, amused but silent, making no move to help her. None of her previ-

[65]

ous experience, as (sort-of) aunt or as (not-so-experienced) detective, had equipped her for this. She didn't want to risk antagonizing her witnesses (and possible suspects).

Finally she decided on the direct approach and appealed to them for help: "I have no idea how to proceed. So how about we just go from right to left?"

The three witnesses considered this and then, as if in telepathic communication, nodded their agreement. It didn't seem as if any type of favouritism was being invoked.

Bella heaved a sigh of relief and turned to the rightmost sister. As middle sister, Molly was not used to being first and was obviously pleased with this change of status. Even Polly's kick to her shin (which she turned aside with long-practiced ease and without even a glance at her sister) failed to deflate her newfound pride or even distract her.

"Polly stop that."

This was the first sound from Lila, but it seemed an automatic response and Molly didn't even bother sticking out her tongue at her younger sister. She could afford to be magnanimous.

"So, Molly," Bella began, "tell me what you did after dinner finished."

"Mummy said to find my stuff so I went to get my marbles but I couldn't find them cause Polly took them."

"I DID NOT!" An indignant Polly jumped up.

"YOU DID TOO!" An equally indignant Molly also jumped up and they stood face to face, noses, at most, an inch apart.

"DID NOT!"
"DID TOO!"
"DID NOT!"

"DID TOO!"

"DID NOT!"

"OK. OK!" Bella managed to interject above the sisters' dids and did-nots. "Why did you think Polly took them?"

"Cause she always does. She's always trying to steal MY marbles cause she always loses when we play and this is her way of getting them cause she can't win them any other way."

Bella tried to forestall the inevitable clash that would follow from this assertion, "But in THIS case – did you see her take them?"

Molly stopped in mid-sentence and considered this twist, "Well not exactly ... "

Again Bella managed to get in before Polly: "Where did you leave them?"

"In the little room – I was playing with them before the meal and then Mummy made me leave them there with my knapsack."

"*I* moved the knapsack."

They all turned to stare at Yolly. "When I picked up my stuff I took Molly's too and put it all by the door so we could make a quick getaway, like Mummy said. But I didn't see the marbles."

Ignoring the reference to Lila's desire to leave the family get-together as soon as possible, Bella focused on Yolly's revelation. Turning back to Molly, she continued her interrogation:

"So, after the meal, you went into the little room. When you didn't see your stuff, what did you do next?"

"I went back to the living room to find Polly. But she wasn't there. I found her in the kitchen."

The questioning went on in this vein for at least another half hour, at which point an exhausted Bella thought she had a somewhat clearer idea of what each of them had done and in what order. She wrote it on a scrap of paper:

Dinner finished
Molly → little room
Polly → kitchen
Yolly → front hall with knapsacks
Molly → kitchen: Molly and Polly start fighting
Lila → kitchen: breaks up fight, sends Molly to front hall and Polly to little room
Yolly goes outside and sits on front porch
Molly puts on shoes and goes back to little room one more time where she finds Polly playing with her toy soldiers
Molly yells at Polly to stop playing and they start fighting
Lila → little room, breaks up fight and sends both of them to front hall
Molly → outside, joins Yolly on porch
Polly can't find one of her socks and goes back to little room, then kitchen, then living room, then front hall, then outside
Lila comes out a few minutes later

When Bella looked at Lila for confirmation on this last point, her cousin finally offered a clarification: "I was looking for the sock. Which I did not find." She looked at her daughter pointedly, then lapsed into silence again.

When she asked if any of them had seen their father, Yolly volunteered the information that he had gone off down the street to smoke his usual after-dinner cigar. Sometime after she got to the porch. He hadn't seen her sitting there plugged into her IPod. He didn't come back until they were all sitting in the car.

When she asked if they had seen any of the others, the replies were not so clear. They had all been focused, with their usual single-mindedness, on their own concerns. Polly thought she had seen Bella and Auntie Gita in the kitchen the first time she was in there. Molly was sure Anna and Carl were in there too, but Polly was just as sure they were not. Yolly saw someone slip around back when she first came out on the porch, didn't know who but thought it might have been the neighbour's sixteen-year-old son sneaking a smoke. The one thing they were all sure about was that Eddie was in the bathroom the whole time. Lila always made them go to the bathroom before they got in the car and this time they couldn't because Eddie was hogging it; they had all seen him go in.

Bella thanked them sincerely for their help and made a grateful exit. She went to the nearest café and ordered the most calming drink they had. As she sipped the camomile tea, she thought about what she had learned so far. It seemed like everyone had had an opportunity, at least, to get to the juice. But when had it actually been spilled?

And where were Jake and Carl all that time? They were obviously next in line to be questioned, but she couldn't see straight any more. She decided to continue the investigation after a good night's sleep.

Brother
When she got to Carl's house the following evening, Bella wasn't surprised by the drop-jaw reaction – she was getting used to it. How had her family become so separate and separated? Had there ever been a time when they'd felt like a real family? Maybe before her father left? Certainly not

since. Zaidy had definitely not become the glue holding the family together!

Jake, recovering more quickly than the others had, invited her in almost graciously. Carl was just finishing dinner and looked up in alarm as his sister entered the kitchen, "What's the matter?" After Bella explained, Carl rolled his eyes: "Give it a rest Bella!"

She couldn't understand his reaction. He was a cop, after all. Were his personal emotions interfering with his professional judgment? Did he just want the whole mess of this past seder to be dead, buried, and forgotten, like all the rest? Did he think she was just being silly? But her nagging feeling wouldn't let her stop. In the end, she made the same appeal as she had to Lila: "Just humour me."

Carl shrugged and rolled his eyes again, but he answered her questions clearly and promptly, almost forgetting to be condescending as his professional persona kicked in. He confirmed what she had learned so far and added a few details of his own. He had helped clear the table, brought dishes and food to the kitchen, seen the girls running around and fighting, seen Eddie enter and leave the bathroom, noted how long he had spent in there (twenty minutes), gone in himself, and then left with Jake. Total time approximately twenty-five minutes. He had not seen George leave. He had not seen Lila leave. He had not seen Anna and Eddie leave. He had seen Molly pick up her knapsack and go out to the porch and, through the briefly opened door, Yolly sitting on the porch. He had not seen the orange juice or orange juice carton. He finished and stared at her, his face impassive and his entire body rigid with 'are we finished with this nonsense now?'

Bella doggedly ignored the disapproval pouring from her brother and turned to Jake, who had not said a word since letting her in. "What about you?" she asked.

"The same."

Bella stared at him, but he didn't seem inclined to elaborate or help in any way. She tried to smile encouragingly, that had no effect either. Obviously, the direct approach was the only one that would produce any results.

"The same as what? Could you be a little more precise?"

"The same as Carl."

This was worse than Lila. Bella couldn't understand it. She had always thought that she and Jake got along relatively well, but he was being way beyond hostile. She looked at Carl, he stared stonily back at her. The tension in the room mounted.

Bella realized she was not going to get anything more. She self-consciously cleared her throat and got to her feet. She managed a "Well I'll be going then" and, before either of the men could move, grabbed her bag and let herself out the front door.

She ran from their house and only slowed down to catch her breath when she was a good two blocks away. She realized she didn't know much about her brother's life or relationship – maybe whatever was going on between them had nothing to do with her or her questions. Or maybe it did. She had no idea. The thoughts swirled round and round in her head, making no sense.

Mother

Bella had come full circle. She was back in her mother's kitchen drinking tea. Gita seemed a little better. She had slept well and the bags under her eyes were a little lighter, a little less obvious.

"Do you remember when you last saw the orange juice carton?"

Her mother turned to her: "Oh Bella, are you still going on about that? Couldn't we just forget it and get on with our lives?"

"But Ma, don't you want to know what happened?"

"Why?"

"Because everyone says they didn't spill the juice. So how did it get there? Someone must have put it there, so why won't that person own up? And you didn't see it when you cleaned up, so it must have gotten there after that, and how could that be? And where'd the juice carton go? It just doesn't make any sense. Someone must be lying but why? Why would anyone lie? I just don't understand it. Unless it wasn't an accident, unless they put it there on purpose, unless they somehow intended for it to kill Zaidy … "

"Who would do that? And why? Why would anyone want to kill Zaidy?"

Bella stopped short, stunned. Up to now, she had been curious about orange juice and little white lies. Now she had moved into a completely different dimension, one that finally scared her: murder? Was she talking about murder? It was the first time Bella had shaped the thought. She froze, covering her mouth. All her investigations had implied it, but she had never actually said it, either out loud or to herself.

MURDER

A scary word.

Especially as the list of suspects was her family.

It meant someone in her family was a murderer. Someone in her very small family – one of ten people she thought she knew well – a murderer.

Her mother looked as if she shared the same thought – her mouth was all twisted, as if she had just swallowed the entire plate of bitter herbs.

"God forbid! Are you crazy? Watch what you're saying Bella!"

Bella went home and thought long and hard. Did she really believe that someone in her family was a murderer? No – she said to herself – it was much more likely that someone, out of absent-mindedness or from wanting to get out of there as soon as possible, had spilled the juice and then not bothered to wipe it up. And her making such a fuss about it and running around "investigating" the "incident" was not going to encourage them to "confess." It was just an accident and the person responsible must already feel bad enough without her making it worse. No wonder Carl had been so annoyed. She went to bed determined to forget the whole thing.

❧

That night she had another visit from Zaidy's ghost. She was sitting in a roller coaster. Two clowns grinned at her from the car in front and, when she turned around, two more grinned at her from behind, their bright painted smiles extending from ear to ear. When she turned back to face forward, she saw the ghost hovering between the two blood-red grins.

Translucent and faintly glowing, the ghost was clearly her departed grandfather. He stared at her so intensely that she felt the beam of concentration from his eyes bore into her. But, even in her sleep, she remembered her decision to forget the whole "incident" and so, resolutely and steadfastly, pulled her head away from the apparition and looked out over the countryside passing below.

The ghost began to get mad – though she was looking the other way, Bella could see that the light around him had changed and was now red and fiery. When she still refused to look his way, he began to growl, a low steady humming kind of growl that grew in volume until it filled her entire being. When it felt like she would explode, she finally turned her head and confronted the ghost, who continued to nail her with his eyes. The growling stopped abruptly. She looked away and the growling began again.

"What do you want from me?" she screamed. But, as she watched, the red light turned to orange and glowed ever more brightly, became a glowing orange circle which enveloped the ghost and slowly began to absorb him.

"No! NO NO NO!!!!!!!" she screamed herself out of the dream.

She tried to fall asleep again, but the image of the ghost dissolving into an orange was there every time she closed her eyes. Finally she got up and tried to distract herself. The trouble was that whenever she stopped moving, the ghost reappeared.

"WHAT DO YOU WANT FROM ME?" she screamed but nobody answered.

"Leave me alone" she muttered, "go and haunt the person who spilled the juice!"

After a week in which the ghost paid her nightly visits, Bella was getting more and more reluctant to fall asleep. Sleep had always been her friend, a refuge from the overstimulating world. Now it had turned into her enemy, lying in wait and ambushing her when she was most vulnerable. She was very very tired and felt like she was sleepwalking through her daily life.

Finally, in desperation, she decided to recreate the seder scene to see if that would dispel Zaidy's ghost and dispatch him to wherever it was that ghosts go. No one in her family was enthusiastic about reconvening at her mother's house, but she was uncharacteristically insistent and, in the end, worried about her, they agreed.

They all sat around the table, in their usual places, the head of the table conspicuously unoccupied. Bella had brought the ritual foods of parsley, horseradish, romaine, shank bone, haroset and egg; she placed these in the centre of the table on the seder plate and the familiar bitter fumes again filled the air. They all looked at Bella, who cleared her throat nervously. She looked at the empty chair at the head of the table and silently invited the ghost to be seated.

She started, "I seem to have become obsessed by Zaidy's death" (no need to mention the ghost) "so I'm grateful that you've all come."

Pause.

"Even though I'm sure it was an accident, someone, one of you, must have spilled the juice."

Pause.

"And someone, I'm sure it was just an accident, forgot to wipe it up."

Pause.

"And Zaidy, for whatever reason he was up, slipped on the juice and banged his head. I'm sure they were all accidents, but I'm going crazy trying to figure out how it happened. I'm not sleeping anymore. I'm going nuts!" (This was probably exactly what they would all think if she told them about the ghost.) "So please please help me here and let's just go through the evening and if everyone can just admit what happened then I can lay this to rest and get on with my life!"

Bella tried not to burst into tears as she finished the longest and most revealing speech she had ever made to her family. The reactions ranged from discomfort to concern. In a family where feelings were barely acknowledged, let alone discussed, this was more startling than if she had ripped off her clothes and danced naked on the table. Maybe more embarrassing as well.

"So let's pretend Zaidy is sitting in his usual place." (Again, no need to mention the ghost which Bella could see settling into the chair.)

"He's just started on his Egypt saga and has been going on for long enough that even he needs to take a breath." (No need to be polite to the ghost – he had been haunting her for long enough – she was not interested in sparing his feelings.)

She reached into her bag and pulled out an orange, which she placed on the seder plate, where it sat among the other foods, bright and colourful and glaringly intense. With the others, she turned towards the sudden gasp near the head of the table and saw a very white Jake struggling to regain his composure.

Bella nodded at him in what she hoped was an encouraging manner, but his mouth remained firmly closed, so she spoke for him.

"Jake started to explain about the orange," she paused and looked at Jake again, who refused to meet her eyes, so she continued, "and Zaidy got upset."

"UPSET!" Jake erupted, "UPSET!"

Bella felt her brother go very still. She kept her eyes on the man who had finally found his tongue but seemed only able to repeat the one word.

"UPSET!!!!!!!" Sputtering and gasping, he kept repeating, "UPSET!! UPSET!!" At last, he found the rest of his words, which came out in a rush, as if they had been waiting for the breach.

"The seder wasn't just his!! It was OURS!! All of us. Not just him, not just his. It wasn't fair, that he got to decide. It wasn't his decision to make. That's what the orange meant, that we were all included. That it belongs to all of us. But he just refused. Point blank. He just refused to even consider it. To ALLOW it. As if he owned it. As if it was his to allow or forbid. But it wasn't just up to him. He didn't OWN it. It is ALL of ours."

In the silence that greeted this eruption, Carl looked at his partner and in a very quiet voice said, "Jake, what have you done?"

Jake tore his glance away from Bella and looked at his partner, the man he had shared his life and home and bed with for the last three years. In a voice breaking and dripping with pleading, he begged him to understand, "Carl, I did this for us. For us. For you and me. This was for us."

Carl, showing no reaction, simply repeated his question in the same still voice: "Jake, what did you do?"

Jake lowered his gaze and looked down at the floor, at the spot where the orange juice had lain, the spot where Zaidy's foot had met with the juice, the spot which had determined the old man's fate.

"I didn't do it!" He said defiantly. "*I* didn't do it!"

Carl continued in the same carefully neutral voice, "What didn't you do?"

Then Jake looked up and met his eyes, "It was God."

Not just Carl, but everyone was now staring at him. Jake looked at them hesitantly, one by one, cleared his throat, and, a little more quietly, repeated:

"I left it up to God."

Bella found her voice and, in what she hoped was a manner similar to her brother's, asked, "What exactly did you leave up to God?"

Jake turned to her, eager to explain, "I left it up to God. To decide."

Bella nodded encouragingly and gestured to Jake to continue, which he did, hungry for approval.

"To decide who was right."

Bella nodded again, willing Jake to be specific. As if he had received her telepathic request, he continued:

"I saw the juice in the fridge and it reminded me of the orange. So I poured some juice, just a very little bit of orange juice, on the floor. Just in case Zaidy should happen to be in the room and should happen to slip."

Bella nodded again and Jake went on.

"And then I saw the marbles under the table. One of the marbles was big and *orange*. It was a sign. So I moved them in front of the juice. Just in case Zaidy should happen to be in the vicinity and should happen to step on the marbles and slip. But I left it up to God to decide."

They all continued to stare at him, mouths still open and mute. Bella was trying to make sense of Jake's words. Thinking out loud, she said:

"But why would Zaidy be in the vicinity? He had nothing to do in the living room in the middle of the night. He was sleeping ... and even if he got up to go to the bathroom he wouldn't come into the living room ..."

She looked over at Jake, who was nodding encouragement, as if she were a good student who had learned the lesson well.

"That's right, he wouldn't ordinarily come into the room. That's why it was up to God. But sometimes God needs help. From us. So I helped."

He turned to Carl, "I borrowed your car and I parked it right outside the living room window. And I turned on the emergency flasher. You know, the one you can hook up on the roof of the car. The flashing *orange* light. Just in case Zaidy saw it and got up to see what it was. And I threw pebbles at the window. Just in case he heard them and saw the light. So he would get up and go to the living room to investigate. And he did."

His righteousness faltered when he registered the increasingly horrified look on Carl's face. But he couldn't stop. Scrambling, he found Bella's eyes. She kept herself very still, trying not to look as sick as she felt.

"And then I left. So God could decide without me influencing the decision. So God could decide between the old ways and the new ones. So God could decide who was right. And who was wrong. Whose turn had come. And whose time had gone. And God did decide."

6. *Beitzah*: the egg. The egg represents the cycle of life: death leading to life, rebirth from the ashes. It is often roasted so that it can also refer back to the Passover sacrifices. Sometimes sacrifices are required before the cycle of life can continue.

BEITZAH

The seder the following year was a subdued affair. For the first time, it was being held at Anna's house. Gita had seemed overwhelmed at the thought of having it; she seemed increasingly overwhelmed by life itself these days. Anna had offered to host it and, surprisingly, Eddie had enthusiastically seconded the offer. When Bella got there, crocuses in hand, her brother-in-law was not only sober, he was in the kitchen working on the food while Anna set the table in the living-room. The atmosphere in the house, though not quite festive, was mellow and pleasant. Anna's anger and unhappiness seemed to have disappeared along with Eddie's drinking.

When Lila arrived, she parked the girls in the living room and wandered into the kitchen where she quietly began to prepare the parsley and bitter herbs while Eddie finished the soup. George came in after parking the car and moved towards the sofa, where Polly got up to make a space for him and then sat back down on his lap.

Carl came shortly afterwards, ushering in his mother, who looked older and sadder than she had a year ago. Carl nodded hello to everyone, but kept his eyes on his mother, who held onto his arm tightly. Carl sat her down at the table and took his own place at the head.

Bella thought of Zaidy and Jake and wondered where they were now. Zaidy's ghost had, thankfully, not reappeared after Jake's confession; perhaps he was, if not at peace, haunting Jake now. Jake had disappeared from their lives. Bella wasn't sure if she would attend the trial, which was scheduled for later that summer, now that Zaidy's ghost had left her in peace.

Bella didn't know if Carl had had any contact with Jake since his astonishing declaration. Carl had very efficiently taken a shaking and lost-looking Jake from the house and to the police station, where he had charged him with criminal negligence leading to death. She knew this only because she had accompanied them to the door and asked her brother what he would do. Since then, Carl had kept his thoughts to himself. He spent more time with his mother and had retreated into an armoured silence.

Eddie and Lila came in from the kitchen and Lila called her family to the table. Bella and Anna took their places as well. The fumes from the bitter herbs seemed less intense this year, leaving room for the freshness of the greens and the sweetness of the haroset.

Carl picked up the haggadah and began the seder.

And a little history:

7. The orange: optional new symbol. The orange represents inclusiveness and diversity. While it first referred to lesbian, gay and other marginalized peoples, it has evolved into a symbol signifying the active participation of women in Jewish rituals.

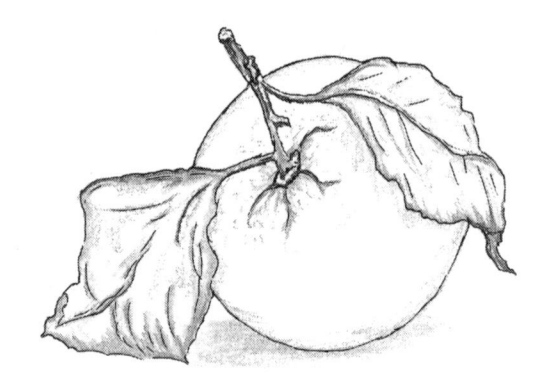

THE ORANGE

Oranges and seders: a strange combination. Or is it? The fact that there is no obvious connection is one of the reasons for its presence: as a jarring reminder to pay attention, to question. It is this very quality that made it a good symbol for Jews who found themselves made invisible at the table. It started out representing lesbian and gay Jews (which is why Jake chose it) before growing to include a much larger group: women.

Homosexuality in Judaism is a complex subject, prickly and controversial. Attitudes of all kinds can be found within the assortment of worldviews that we call "Judaism", attitudes ranging from complete acceptance to complete rejection.

Opinions are no less diverse regarding the place of women in Judaism. While many Jewish women are happy and satisfied with their roles, others find these so problematic that they have renounced Judaism altogether. Still other women find themselves somewhere in between, belonging yet not belonging, struggling, out of place, out of sorts, but still trying to find or create a space that fits.

The orange symbolizes all these desires, histories, struggles, invisibilities, and demands: of lesbians, of gays, and of women. Such a lot of meaning for such a little fruit.

It was chosen almost by accident, as a replacement for a different food. A woman's group in Berkeley had put a crust of bread on their seder plate. They did it to represent the way lesbians were perceived and treated within Judaism. But bread is such a taboo food during Passover that many felt that, instead of highlighting the problem, it negated the whole holiday.

Susannah Heschel, a Jewish activist committed to the Jewish tradition but equally committed to making necessary changes to that tradition, heard about the bread. She liked the idea of focusing attention on the position of lesbians and other marginalized Jews, but found the bread itself too extreme. She wanted something that allowed for and acknowledged some amount of inclusion. What she came up with was the orange.

Perhaps she was influenced by the qualities and history of the orange and its relatives. The entire citrus family is, by its nature, ambiguous. A citrus seed can grow into any kind of citrus plant – orange seeds do not necessarily produce orange trees. When the ancient Jews moved to other lands, they had to plant many citrus seeds to be sure of getting the pure citron ("etrog") they needed for the holiday of Sukkot. In fact, their plantings may even have been responsible for the spread of the citrus family.

Heschel also liked the fact that oranges contained seeds that had to be spat out; she compared this to the homophobia that did not allow Jewish lesbians and gay men to sit comfortably at the table.

Hmmm... unpredictable, ambiguous... a problematic purity. The symbol fit very well with the position of marginalized Jews. Even more so with the position of women in Judaism: sometimes exalted for being "spiritually purer", and so excluded from many rituals and practices because of their "spirituality"… and sometimes excluded simply because they are women and their very physicality renders them "impure".

How did we even get from lesbians and other marginalized people to women? That is the stuff of urban legends: in the years that followed Heschel's first orange, the stories proliferated and changed focus. Heschel disappeared and a nameless hostile male rabbi made his way onto a stage, from where he pronounced the unsuitability of women performing sacred acts such as reading from the Torah scrolls, acts so out of place that they were like an orange on a seder plate. The orange's subsequent appearance on seder plates could then be seen as an in-your-face response to the rabbi. This version is the most widespread, the one most people have heard.

Perhaps Heschel was also inspired by the history of the other foods on the plate. Most of them joined long after the holiday was first celebrated. Some were substitutions due to unavailability of foods in different climates and regions, but some were brought to the table intentionally, in order to bring about a change in awareness. For instance, the lamb shank was introduced by the rabbis because the ancient sacrifice ritual (the "Paschal lamb") was no longer possible after the Jerusalem Temple was destroyed in 70CE. Rather than cancel the holiday, the rabbis decided to use a symbolic food to reenvision the ritual, while inviting rememberance of the former sacrifice.

When vegetarian Jews make their own substitutions today, with a "Paschal yam" or a beet, they are following in the rabbis' footsteps. The actual food is not as important as what it refers to, and its main purpose is as a stimulus for discussion.

By its lack of obvious connection, the orange is very effective in this regard. Most of the women I interviewed during my doctoral research placed it on their seder plates precisely for that reason. One explained that she also put it there to counter her invisibility, that, because of its hard-to-overlook appearance, she felt like she was inserting itself into the centre of the ritual:

> ... all these elders, males, leading the service, and there I am, plonk with the orange... it says, pretty clearly, in my act of putting it on the seder plate, that I'm there, and that's really the crux of it. I'm there and you're going to have to deal with me.

Jewish rituals are in transition. The seder is constantly changing, as it has throughout its history. The orange has made some inroads, but is still far from an accepted, or even well-known, component. However, seder plates are already being created with a place for the orange and haggadahs that include references to the orange are being written for a general audience.

Who knows what the future will bring? Perhaps the orange will disappear because it is no longer needed at an egalitarian seder that welcomes and celebrates all kinds of diversities, including sexual orientation.

Perhaps it will disappear because there is no room for it at a seder that has re-established rigid boundaries clearly marking inclusions and exclusions.

Perhaps the orange will remain on the plate but lose its visibility as it fades into the familiar.

And perhaps, at least for the foreseeable future, the orange will remain on the plate, visible and bright and glowing, a yearly beacon of hope and inspiration. Only time will tell…

※

[For a more complete and serious discussion, see my dissertation *Transforming rituals: contemporary Jewish women's seders* (Concordia University, Canada: 2006).]

Sonia Zylberberg lives in Montreal. She teaches at Dawson College and reads mystery novels in her spare time. You can contact her at soniaz.orange@gmail.com or visit her website www.soniaz.weebly.com.